The Curious Little Dolphin

Written by Ariane Chottin
Adapted by Patricia Jensen
Illustrations by Olivier Raquois

Published by The Reader's Digest Association Limited
London ❖ New York ❖ Sydney ❖ Montreal

It was a beautiful summer's day and Sophie, a baby dolphin, was swimming with her mother and her aunt in the deep blue sea.

She flipped up to the surface of the water for air but made sure she stayed very close to her mother for she was still a very little dolphin, only a few days old.

'Sophie,' said her mother. 'You must take care and never swim alone for the sea can be a very dangerous place for young dolphins on their own.'

But, as Sophie looked around her, she saw all the other young dolphins having a wonderful time in the water. They rode the waves, they flipped and turned somersaults. They looked so happy!

'I'd love to do that too,' sighed Sophie. 'I want to play with them and dance in the waves.'

'Not yet,' said her mother. 'You must be patient and stay close to me. We're about to set out on a difficult and long journey south where the waters are much warmer. Once we get there you'll have the time of your life!'

At sunset that evening the dolphins set off for the warmth of the south. In the midst of the group were the two youngest – Sophie and also Splash who was just a few days older than her. The two soon became close friends.

Both of them were extremely excited and flipped and bounced through the water.

'Stay with the group! Don't swim away,' urged Sophie's mother. 'The sea's full of dangers! If the shark sees you, he'll gobble you up for dinner!'

'But just wait till we get to the south,' whispered Sophie to Splash. 'Then we can go off and explore everything all by ourselves. It'll be such fun!'

The dolphins swam and swam till at last the waters were warmer. The sea around them shimmered and brightly coloured little fish darted through the seaweed and corals. The two little dolphins couldn't believe their eyes; they thought they were in fairyland!

'Please, oh please, can we go and play now?' Sophie asked her mother.

'Wait a little longer. We're all tired from the journey. You'll have plenty of time to play tomorrow,' said her mother. But the two young dolphins were so impatient, they found it very difficult to settle down and rest.

When the sun rose the next morning, Sophie's mother had to go and hunt for food.

'Stay here with your aunt,' she told Sophie. 'I'll take you both exploring when I get back.'

But Sophie and Splash had spotted a rocky island in the distance and they wanted to investigate. As soon as their aunt's back was turned, the two naughty little dolphins slipped away from the group and raced off through the water together.

It was brilliant! The sun shone through the water creating huge circles of light and the two friends danced in the beams, then sped off into the shadows playing hide-and-seek among the rocks.

Then Sophie looked down and spotted a cave. 'Look,' she called to Splash. 'Let's go and see what we can find.'

The mouth of the cave glistened in the sunlight and a shoal of little fish passed them and swam through. 'Come on,' urged Sophie. 'Let's follow them inside!'

Sophie and Splash swam into the cave. This was a shimmering, sparkling world they had never seen before! They looked excitedly at the red anemones waving their tiny tentacles. They watched the black-and-yellow clown fish dart back and forth. But, as they swam deeper into the cave, the water became darker and darker.

'What's that over there?' Splash asked nervously. 'I think I can see two shining eyes...'

Sophie looked up just in time to see a huge shark swimming rapidly towards them.

'Oh, no!' she cried. 'A shark and he's got enormous teeth!'

The two turned tail and fled for their lives. Through the dark cave waters they sped back out into the light. The shark swiftly pursued them with an evil smile on his ugly face.

'Help, help!' the two little dolphins called in desperation.

Within seconds, the big dolphins raced to their rescue and surrounded them. They were safe! The shark turned angrily and swam away.

Two mothers were extremely cross and Sophie and Splash were very sad and sorry. But the parents soon forgave them. 'It's hard not to be curious when there are so many things to see and do,' they said. 'But from now on ...'

'We'll do them together,' said Sophie. 'It's much safer that way!'

All about ... DOLPHINS

MAMMALS LIKE US

Although they live in water, dolphins are not fish. They are mammals, which means that they breathe air and nurse their young. Baby dolphins stay with their mothers for more than a year.

COMING UP FOR AIR

Dolphins breathe through an opening, called a blow-hole, at the top of their heads. The blow-hole opens to let air in and out and closes when the dolphin's head is under water.

FACT FILE

KEEN HEARING

A dolphin's ears are very small - just two tiny holes, one behind each eye. Nevertheless, dolphins hear ten times better than people do!

DOLPHIN-SPEAK

Dolphins are extremely intelligent and communicate with each other by whistles, grunts and hums. Some scientists even think that mother dolphins sing lullabies to their babies.

▶ Dolphins can learn lots of tricks and are popular performers at aquariums. They can be trained to jump through hoops, find objects underwater and take fish from their trainer's hand.

▶ Dolpins are very gentle. They never attack people. In fact, they have even been known to help tired swimmers by pulling them back to shallow water.

The Curious Little Dolphin is a Little Animal Adventures book
published by Reader's Digest Young Families, Inc.
by arrangement with Éditions Nathan, Paris, France

Written by Ariane Chottin
Adapted by Patricia Jensen
Illustrations by Olivier Raquois
Notebook artwork © Paul Bommer

This edition was adapted and published in 2008 by
The Reader's Digest Association Limited
11 Westferry Circus, Canary Wharf, London E14 4HE

® Reader's Digest, the Pegasus logo and Reader's Digest Young Families
are registered trademarks of
The Reader's Digest Association, Inc.

We are committed to both the quality of our products
and the service we provide to our customers.
We value your comments, so please feel free to contact us on
08705 113366 or via our website at:
www.readersdigest.co.uk
If you have any comments or suggestions about the content of our books,
you can contact us at:
gbeditorial@readersdigest.co.uk

Printed in China

Book code: 637-009 UP0000-2
ISBN: 978 0 276 44237 7